Sargent, Dave and Pat

Ding Bat

JF
SAR

DATE DUE			

10/13

Dave and Pat Sargent are longtime residents of Prairie Grove, Arkansas. Dave, a fourth-generation dairy farmer, began writing in early December 1990, and Pat, a former teacher, began writing shortly after. They enjoy the outdoors and have a real love for animals.

Ding Bat

By

Dave and Pat Sargent

Illustrated by
Jane Lenoir

Ozark Publishing, Inc.
P.O. Box 228
Prairie Grove, AR 72753

Library of Congress Cataloging-in-Publication Data

Sargent, Dave, 1941-
  Ding Bat / by Dave and Pat Sargent ; illustrated by
Jane Lenoir.
      p. cm.
Summary: Smaller than most bats, Ding Bat has lost
his confidence until a new cow friend convinces him
that he can lead all the other bats safely out of a storm.
  ISBN 1-56763-529-6 (hardback)—ISBN 1-56763-
530-X (pbk.)
  [1. Bats—Fiction. 2. Cows—Fiction. 3. Self-confi-
dence—Fiction.] I. Sargent, Pat, 1936- II. Lenoir,
Jane, 1946—ill. III. Title.
  PZ7.S2465 Df 2000
  [Fic]—dc21
                                        00-011307

Printed in the United States of America

iv

Inspired by

the many times we have visited the huge caves known as Carlsbad Caverns, in New Mexico, and watched bats go out to feed and come back in. They are always on schedule.

Dedicated to

all kids who are curious about bats. We know several kids who are afraid of bats. This may be wise since bats can carry rabies. If one scratches or bites you, you are in for a series of shots!

Foreword

Ding Bat is smaller than most bats. He lives and travels with a big circus. When the circus train wrecks, Ding finds himself a new *temporary* home but all of his new-found friends tease him and make fun of him.

Ding loses his self-confidence and, of course, this causes him to lose his very necessary radar and sonar powers. He keeps bumping into things!

Contents

Ding Bat

If you would like to have the authors of the Animal Pride Series visit your school, free of charge, call 1-800-321-5671 or 1-800-960-3876.

One

No Radar! No Sonar!

"Hey, Ding Bat, wake up!" a voice shouted. "The sun is down, and nobody can leave until you move out of the way."

The little bat opened his eyes and tried to see up the long, narrow passageway.

"Oh my," he groaned. "It's almost dark and time to get up."

"Out of the way, Ding!" another voice ordered.

"Hey, fellows," Ding pleaded, "I didn't find my way back home

1

until after daylight. You know my radar instinct does not work good. Last night I spent more time bumping into things than finding food."

Giggles from his fourteen new-found friends echoed within the rock cave. Ding shook his head, wriggled his pointed ears, and opened his mouth, exposing two long fangs.

The very tired little Ding Bat slowly turned from his upside-down sleeping position and unfolded the leathery skin between his body and arms. He was aware of bruises, but he felt that he would be able to fly.

I'm a little sore, he thought, but hitting a light pole is not going to stop me! But I do need to return to the site of the wrecked circus train so they can take care of me.

Ding began crawling up the crack in the rocks. Soon he heard his friends following him upward. They were still complaining.

A moment later, he was soaring toward Farmer John's Place.

"Tonight will be a better night," he muttered. "Accuracy is my aim, and insects are the game. I am determined to get a full tummy without having a wreck."

Suddenly he veered downward. The wind screamed in his ears as he drew nearer to the target.

Thud! Ding's little body hit a fence post and slid to the ground.

Moments later, Ding was again airborne. Soaring around the light on Farmer John and Molly's front porch, he felt that he could not miss dinner this time. As he turned to make a second pass through the area, Molly stepped out on the porch.

Whap! Ding hit the lady on the side of her head, and she screamed.

"Molly!" Farmer John yelled from within the house. "What's going on out there? Are you okay?"

"I - I - think so," she muttered. "It feels like I was just hit in the head with a stick or a bat or something. But I'll be all right."

As Molly slowly walked back in the house, Ding shook his head and wriggled his arms. Yes, he decided. I, too, will be okay.

Once again airborne, the little bat knew that something alive was below him, and he nose-dived downward at top speed. He grinned and giggled as he approached the target.

"Hey, friends," Ding shrieked. "Look at me now. My radar instinct is working tonight."

But seconds later, Ding again hit the ground.

"Oh," he groaned. "Did I hit a brick wall or what?"

"No," a deep voice replied.

"You collided with the backside of a young cow named Fancy Fannie." She giggled and added, "That's me."

"Oh," Ding murmured. "Sorry about that. I hope I didn't hurt you."

"I'm fine," Fancy Fannie said. "What were you trying to do?"

The little bat did not answer.

"Are you hurt?" Fancy asked.

For a moment, little Ding Bat considered playing dead. He hoped that the light from the moon would not be bright enough for the large animal to see him. He was so embarrassed about bragging only seconds ago that he did not want anybody to see him. But the Jersey was concerned about this little thing.

"What's your name, little one?" Fancy asked in a kind tone of voice. "I'm sorry that I was in your way."

She nudged the little bat with her nose, and he groaned and looked up at her.

"Nothing is hurt but my pride," Ding said. "Your apology is embarrassing me in front of my friends."

"Oh dear," Fancy whispered. "I'm sorry!"

"You just did it again!" the little bat growled.

Through foggy vision, he stared up at two great big brown eyes and a huge, damp nose.

"Hello," he finally said meekly. "My name is Ding Bat. You may call me Ding for short. I - I - I'm sorry that I ran into you."

"No harm done," Fancy replied. "I'm not hurt, but I'm not sure about you. You look a little beat up."

The little bat suddenly began to cry. Ding was so disappointed and so embarrassed with his night's performance that he thought his heart would break. Big tears rolled down his thin snout and fell to the ground.

Fancy said, "Tell me about your problem, Ding. Perhaps I can help."

Ding Bat wiped the tears from his face with one hand and then looked up into Fancy Fannie's big brown eyes.

"I'm a bat," little Ding quietly explained, "and bats are famous for excellence in both radar and sonar accuracy. Our eyes are not that good, but we have this special gift that tells us where everything is." He paused a moment before adding, "We never miss!"

"Hmmm, I think I understand," Fancy moaned. "Your radar and sonar is not working. Am I right?"

"No. Mine's not working," Ding said. "Boy, is it not working! I thought you were a mosquito."

Fancy chuckled softly and said, "Yes, Ding, my little friend, you do have a problem."

Ding sniffled and squeaked, "What am I going to do, Fancy? I can't find food to eat or my wrecked circus train or anything."

"Hmmm," Fancy pondered. "You just relax a minute. Why don't you sit on my back where you will be safe while I do some thinking?"

Two

I ~~Can't~~ Can!

For thirty minutes or so, Ding sat on Fancy Fannie's back as she slowly paced back and forth inside the corral. After several minutes had passed, Fancy stopped pacing and asked, "Ding, think hard. Did you have a bump on the head before you lost your radar?"

"I never bumped my head or anything else," Ding Bat sputtered, "until after I lost it!"

"Hmmm," Fancy thoughtfully hummed and began to pace again.

Suddenly the sound of squeaks and giggles caught the attention of Fancy, and she stopped and looked around.

"What's that noise I hear?" she muttered.

"Oh, just ignore them," Ding growled. "My friends think my boo-boos are funny. This morning they went home without me, and the sun was already up when I stumbled in our cave to go to bed."

"Have they always made fun of you?" Fancy asked.

"Well," Ding said hesitantly, "I haven't known them very long, but everybody has always treated me a little differently. I am smaller than an average bat, and it takes me a little longer to learn things. I guess that's why they call me Ding Bat."

"Oh. I understand," Fancy murmured.

Ding sputtered, "Well, I'm glad you understand because I don't!"

"Get off my back, Ding," she said. "I need to see you while I explain something very important."

The little bat flew from her back and landed on the ground in front of her. He looked up into her big brown eyes. He could feel the warmth of caring from a true friend.

"I'm so sorry, Fancy Fannie," he quietly murmured. "I know it hurt when I ran into you, and you didn't even make fun or yell at me."

The cow gently nudged him with her nose.

"No, Ding," she chuckled. "You didn't hurt me. I feel bad that you are misunderstood by your friends. I think that you've been teased about your size and abilities for so long that you've buried your self-confidence in a deep hole called 'I can't do this,' and now you truly believe that you can't." She paused a moment before quietly declaring, "Your radar's not really broken, little one. It's just stuck in the 'I can't' mode."

"It is?" the little bat asked.

"Yes," Fancy said with a smile. "It is. Your newfound friends and acquaintances just convinced you that it was broken."

"Wow!" Ding Bat sighed. "I'm sure glad of that!" He paused for a moment before asking, "But, Fancy, just how can I get my accuracy out of 'I can't'?"

Fancy again smiled.

"When you really need this gift," she said quietly, "it will be there for you, Ding. Stop trying so hard, and you will not miss your intended target."

Suddenly the stillness of night was shattered by a crash from a bolt of lightning, immediately followed by the deep bellow of thunder. Before the two had a chance to seek shelter, huge raindrops were pelting the countryside. And seconds later, hail stones began to fall from the dark, heavy cloud overhead.

Three

It Takes Confidence!

All through the nightmarish howl and roar of the storm, Ding heard shouts of pain and confusion from his friends as they struggled to survive. Fancy's big body served as a shield for the little bat as he tried to see the location of his bat friends.

The hail stopped as suddenly as it had started, but rain and high winds continued to batter the farm.

"I must go and help my friends find shelter," Ding yelled. "Are you sure that my radar is not broken?"

"Absolutely!" Fancy Fannie bellowed above the howl of the wind. "Your accuracy is perfect. Just pull it out from 'I can't' and put it in 'I can.' Go now!"

Ding Bat felt the raindrops pound against his body as he soared upward. The roaring wind shoved him off course several times, but instinct immediately corrected the boo-boo.

"Timmy, Tommy, Sarah!" he yelled as he fought his way through the storm. "Andy, Angie, Richard! Follow me!"

Another streak of lightning filled the sky, followed by the roar of deafening thunder.

"Billy, Betty, Mary Sue!" he screamed. "Teddy, Todd, Milly! Come with me!"

Ding was gaining confidence. By now, he was flying so fast that he no longer noticed the hard droplets of water pounding against his body.

"My friends need my help," he muttered through clenched fangs, "and my radar is out of 'I can't' and working great."

He circled the entire area near the corral once more as the wind whipped against his frail-looking wings. The glint of determination in his eyes did not waver as he called once more upon his instinct.

"Jimmy and Joe!" he bellowed. "Fall in behind me!" And even though he couldn't see them, Ding knew that all fourteen of his friends were right behind him as he flew through the storm toward home.

At the entrance to their cave, Ding stepped back and allowed each one to enter the safety of the cave. He smiled and nodded as Billy, the fourteenth member of his crew, entered the dry sanctuary.

For nearly two hours, the little bat friends celebrated with dancing and singing.

"Little Ding saved us from the storm," they chanted. "He's our very best friend. He saved our lives. Our Ding Bat is also our hero!"

The littlest bat was once again embarrassed. But this time his heart felt warm and happy. Thank you, Fancy Fannie, he silently mused. You were right. And now I'm in the "I can" mode and I intend to stay there! He turned upside down and folded his arms to sleep.

I must always remember the importance of self-confidence and never ever lose my accuracy again.

Hmmm. I am one fine and accurate little bat!

Four

Bat Facts

The bat is the only mammal capable of sustained flight. Bats are divided into two suborders—larger bats or megabats and smaller bats or microbats—and seventeen families. One of these families includes all megabats (more than 150 species); the other sixteen families are microbats. In all, 850 to 900 species of bats exist, far more than in any other mammalian order except the order of rodents, and bats probably exceed even rodents in total abundance.

Bats are believed to have originated in the early Eocene Epoch. The oldest known fossil bat is about 60 million years old. They are worldwide, except in the Arctic Zone and remote oceanic islands.

The megabats include the largest bats, the giant "flying foxes" of Africa, Australo-Malaysia, and India. They are so called because of their long, dog-like muzzles. The biggest, a megabat inhabiting Java, has a wingspan of 5 feet, 6 inches and a body length of 16.7 inches.

Many species of megabats are smaller than the microbats. The distinction between the suborders is based on tooth form and skeletal differences rather than size alone.

The smallest microbat, Kitti's hog-nosed bat of western Thailand, is only 1.1 to 1.3 inches long and weighs about 0.07 ounces, making it one of the tiniest of mammals.

Among living vertebrates, true flight is unique to bats and birds. Unlike most birds, however, bats are able to fly at relatively low speeds with extreme maneuverability. The wing is a thin, fleshy membrane supported near its leading edge by the greatly elongated bones of the fore-limb and second finger, and toward the tip and rear by the even more attenuated third, fourth, and fifth fingers. It is attached along the midline of the trunk and outward-directed legs, and in some species it extends between legs and tail.

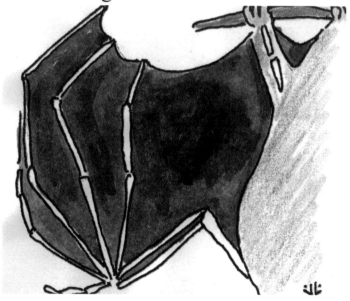

Only the first finger, or thumb, is free, and in most bats it alone is clawed, together with the toes. This helps bats to vary the convexity of the wings dramatically and thus vary their aerodynamic lift.

All microbats navigate—and most target their prey—by echolocation. This is the pulsed emission of high-frequency sounds that are reflected back as echoes to a bat's ears from surrounding surfaces, indicating the position, relative distance, and even the character of objects in its environment. In this sense microbats "see" acoustically. This allows them to navigate in total darkness. The sound pulses are generated in the larynx, and in different species are emitted either from the mouth or the nostrils.

Most microbats are nocturnal. During the day they rest in caves, crevices, hollow trees, foliage, hiding places beneath rocks or bark, and in buildings.

WHITE TENT BATS ON LEAF-
GREY TENT BAT

Being nocturnal gives bats many advantages, such as greatly reduced competition for insects and other food items, substantial freedom from attack, and protection from overheating and dehydration.

Megabats use vision rather than acoustics for orientation. The eyes of megabats are also relatively larger than those of microbats. No bat is blind, however, and even echolocating microbats may use gross visual landmarks for homing during flight. Most megabats are fruit eaters.

FRUIT BAT

Still others in both groups consume flower parts or extract the nectar from flowering plants by means of greatly elongated tongues, aiding cross-pollination of the plants in the process. Most bats are insectivorous and are able to catch their prey in flight or to seek out stationary insects on foliage or other surfaces.

Some of the larger leaf-nosed bats as well as members of one Eurasian family are carnivorous or omnivorous; they attack small amphibians, lizards, birds, mice, and even other bats, in addition to consuming insects and fruit.

GOTHIC BAT

LARGE-
    EARED
GOTHIC

Closely related to the leaf-nosed bats are the true vampires of the American Tropics, which subsist entirely on blood freshly drawn from small wounds inflicted on mostly warm-blooded prey such as fowl, cattle, horses, swine, and occasionally human beings.

VAMPIRE BAT

At least three species of bats supplement their diets with small fish, which are caught as the flying bats drag their enlarged feet and claws just beneath the water surface.

The gestation periods of bats are relatively long, ranging from about 44 days to 8 months in various species. Few produce more than a single offspring each year, and the young tend to mature slowly.

Some larger species of mega-bats and the smaller vampire bat have survived in zoos for 20 years. Among the microbats banded and released in the wild, many have been recaptured after years of freedom. The record is a bat recovered 31 years after it was marked and released in New England.

Because of their size and numbers, the larger fruit bats of Eurasia can be a menace when they invade fruit orchards. The greatest adverse effect of all bats is the transmission of disease, especially rabies, to domesticated animals. Most species of bats inhabiting the United States and Canada have been reported at one time and place or another to be infected with rabies.